For
Caz

First published 1994 by Walker Books Ltd
87 Vauxhall Walk, London SE11 5HJ

This edition published 2007

2 4 6 8 10 9 7 5 3

This book has been typeset in AT Arta.

Printed in China

British Library Cataloguing in Publication Data:
a catalogue record for this book is
available from the British Library.

ISBN 978-1-4063-0989-8

www.walkerbooks.co.uk

Pointy-hatted Princesses

Nick Sharratt

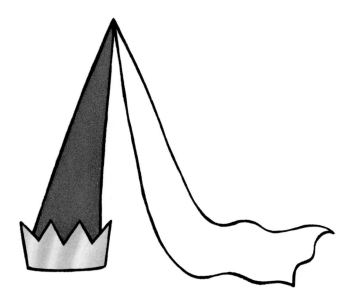

WALKER BOOKS
AND SUBSIDIARIES
LONDON • BOSTON • SYDNEY • AUCKLAND

It was
raining.

Princess Maud
was bored.

Princess Bridget
started to fidget.

Princess Dawn
gave a yawn.

Princess Grace
pulled a face.

Princess Trudy was REALLY moody.

Then the sun
came out and
they all went,
"HOORAY!"

and ran
outside ...

to play football.

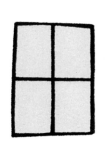